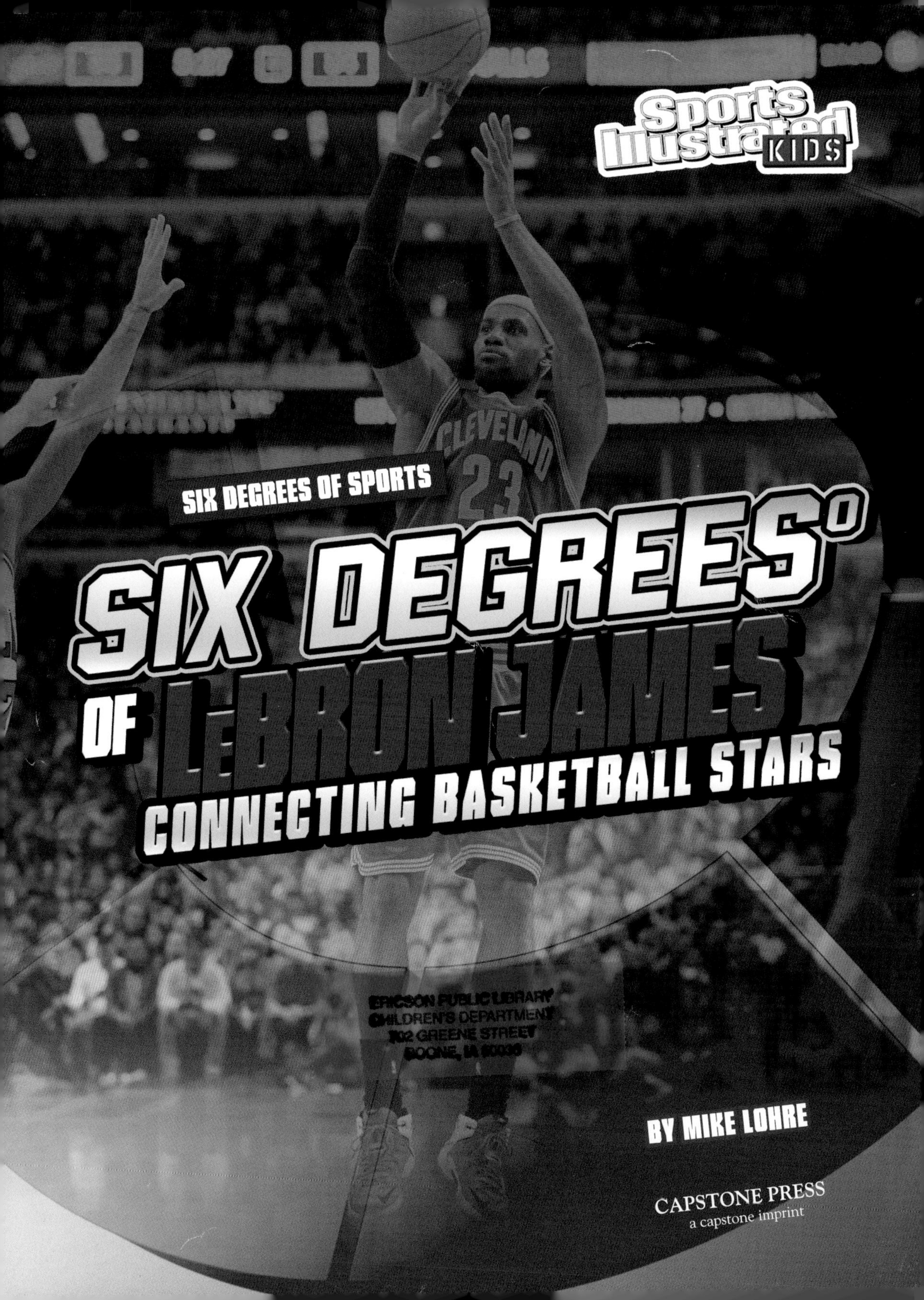

Sports Illustrated KIDS

SIX DEGREES OF SPORTS

SIX DEGREES°
OF LEBRON JAMES
CONNECTING BASKETBALL STARS

BY MIKE LOHRE

CAPSTONE PRESS
a capstone imprint

Sports Illustrated Kids Six Degrees of Sports are published by Capstone Press,
1710 Roe Crest Drive, North Mankato, Minnesota 56003. www.capstonepub.com

Library of Congress Cataloging-in-Publication Data
Cataloging information on file with the Library of Congress
ISBN 978-1-4914-2144-4

Editorial Credits

Nate LeBoutillier, editor; Ted Williams, designer; Eric Gohl, media researcher;
Katy LaVigne, production specialist

Photo Credits

Corbis: Bettmann, cover (Allen, Naismith), 6 (Allen), 10 (bottom), 11; Getty Images: Hulton Archive, 6 (Naismith),
NBAE/NBA Photo Library, 24 (Brown), 29 (bottom); Newscom: EFE/Craig Lassig, 16, MCT/Joshua C. Cruey,
18 (Davis), UPI/Nell Redmond, 22; Sports Illustrated: Al Tielemans, 8 (top), Andy Hayt, cover (Jordan), 9, 17
(top), 30 (Abdul-Jabbar), 35, Bill Frakes, 18 (background), 19, 20, 30 (Anthony), Bob Rosato, 13, 16 (background),
21 (bottom), Damian Strohmeyer, 12 (background), 14 (top), 27, 40 (top), David E. Klutho, cover (James), 1,
4–5, 6 (James, background), 7, 10 (background), 18 (Hibbert), 24 (Allen), 30 (Love), 32 (bottom), 33, 34 (bottom),
Hy Peskin, 12 (Cousy), 14 (bottom), John Biever, 18 (Mourning), John G. Zimmerman, cover (Chamberlain),
6 (Chamberlain), 10 (top), 18 (Russell), John W. McDonough, cover (Wade), 8 (bottom), 12 (Rondo, Kidd), 17
(bottom), 21 (top), 24 (Curry, Lillard, background), 25, 26 (all), 30 (Durant, Bryant, background), 31, 32 (top,
background), 34 (top), 36 (Nowitzki, Nash, Parker, Ming, Ginobili, background), 37, 38 (all), 39, 40 (bottom),
Manny Millan, 6 (Jordan), 12 (Johnson), 18 (Mutumbo, Ewing), 23 (top), 24 (Miller, Bird), 28, 30 (Malone), Richard
Meek, 23 (bottom), Robert Beck, 36 (Divac), 41, Simon Bruty, 6 (Wade), 12 (Rubio), Tony Triolo, 12 (Maravich), 15,
Walter Iooss Jr., 29 (top)

Design Elements

Shutterstock

Source Notes

Page 11: James Naismith. *Basketball: It's Origin and Development.* New York: Association Press, 1941. Page
14: Baxter Holmes. "Rajon Rondo, Celtics handle the Pistons." BostonGlobe. com. 10 March 2014. www.
bostonglobe.com/sports/2014/03/09. Page 23: JT Richard. "Bill Russell: The Greatest Shot Blocker of All Time."
BleacherReport.com. 6 Aug. 2010. www.bleacherreport.com/articles. Page 38: Dan Favale. "Kobe Bryant Calls
Dirk Nowitzki, Pau Gasol Best Foreign Players Ever." BleacherReport.com. 23 June 2013. http://bleacherreport.
com/articles/1681920. Page 40: *David Stern and Yao Ming. NBA.com.* Video. 19 Nov. 2014. www.nba.com/video/
channels/nba_tv/2012/10/14/david-stern-yao-ming-full-china-presser.nba/.

Printed in the United States of America in Stevens Point, Wisconsin.
112014   008479WZS15

TABLE OF CONTENTS

REMINDS ME OF . . .

LeBron James skies for the rebound, comes back to Earth, and turns. A tall mix of dancer, sprinter, and magician, he makes his way to the basket. Again he takes to the airways, this time to cuff-dunk a basket-shaking work of art. The fact that you're in disbelief shows that he has done more than just score two points. He has brought you to your feet—or to your knees—and coaxed a roar from your throat—unless he has left you speechless. And whether you say out loud or not, what you're thinking is, *I've never seen that before.*

But someone has seen it before. This is just about the time your father says, *"Reminds me of Air Jordan."*

To which your grandfather, once upon a time, might have said, *"Reminds me of Wilt the Stilt."*

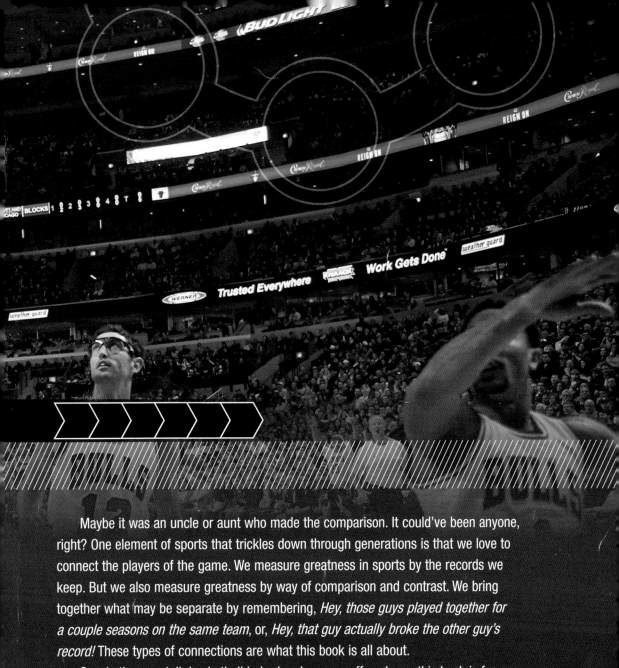

Maybe it was an uncle or aunt who made the comparison. It could've been anyone, right? One element of sports that trickles down through generations is that we love to connect the players of the game. We measure greatness in sports by the records we keep. But we also measure greatness by way of comparison and contrast. We bring together what may be separate by remembering, *Hey, those guys played together for a couple seasons on the same team*, or, *Hey, that guy actually broke the other guy's record!* These types of connections are what this book is all about.

So whether you talk basketball in barbershops or coffee shops, this book is for you. Whether you strike up debate in back rooms, parlor rooms, living rooms, chat rooms, or lunchrooms, on the streets or in the bleachers, with your friends or foes or teachers, this Six Degrees of Sports book is for you. Please enjoy it, and make your own connections.

CHAPTER ONE

MICHAEL JORDAN
Played and won championships in Wade's hometown of Chicago.

DWYANE WADE
Teammate of LeBron James on championship Miami Heat in 2012 and 2013.

WILT CHAMBERLAIN
Revered as most dominant scorer in game's history, along with Jordan.

SIX DEGREES
OF LeBRON JAMES

PHOG ALLEN
Longtime KU icon coached Wilt in Chamberlain's Jayhawk days.

JAMES NAISMITH
Inventor of the game of basketball, and Allen's coach at Kansas University.

THE ROOTS OF ROUNDBALL

Basketball is a cooperative sport with five players competing for each team. Still the game offers enough freedom on the court for any one player to sometimes rise above and be recognized as the best individual player in the game. To achieve that greatness, a player needs ability but also the drive to work hard to improve each year.

HEIGHT: 6-8   WEIGHT: 250 lbs.
BORN: 12/30/1984 in Akron, Ohio
SCOUTING REPORT: Nearly unstoppable and the most feared player in the game today. Can handle ball, score, defend, block, and lead. Has all the tools for dominance.

In today's National Basketball Association (NBA), most agree that the best basketball player on the planet is ▶ **LeBron James**. The Cleveland Cavaliers star is a four-time league Most Valuable Player (MVP), and he won NBA championships with the Miami Heat in 2012 and 2013.

LeBron handles the ball like a guard, but he is 6-foot-8 and 250 pounds. Although his natural position is forward, he has the skills to play anywhere on the court. He's an imposing defender who has caused many players on fast breaks to cringe as he chases them down from behind to block a shot. Swat!

What defines greatness? For LeBron, it's the ability to use his superior skills on both offense and defense in service of team basketball. LeBron represents a new type of player that James Naismith could have hardly imagined when he invented the game.

Like LeBron, ▶ **Dwyane Wade** was drafted into the NBA in 2003. While the two would eventually play together, Wade spent his first seven seasons in Miami without LeBron. Wade showed he could lead a team to the promised land when he led the Heat to its first title in

HEIGHT: 6-4   WEIGHT: 220 lbs.
BORN: 1/17/1982 in Chicago, Ill.
SCOUTING REPORT: One of the most creative shooting guards in the game. Can create own shot. Powerful going to hoop. Good defender.

2006. In the Finals Wade averaged 34.7 points per game and captured the 2006 NBA Finals MVP award.

From the shooting guard position, Wade scores with an arsenal of moves. His drives and improvised shots are often spectacular. Wade has routinely left fans and opponents saying, *Did you see that?* Wade is also an excellent defender and leads the NBA in all-time blocked shots for players 6-foot-4 or less.

Wade was born in Chicago, home of the Bulls. The most legendary player in Bulls history—and possibly NBA history—was none other than ▶ **Michael "Air" Jordan**. Air Jordan was nicknamed for a magnificent leaping ability that allowed him to seemingly hang in mid-air.

Jordan helped Chicago to six NBA titles and was a 14-time All-Star. Countless stories have created his legend of greatness. One such story dates to when Jordan famously won the NBA Slam Dunk Contest in 1988. You can imagine this in slow motion if you wish: At full speed Jordan raced down the court and jumped from the free throw line. He soared, hung, floated, and stuck out his tongue for the winning slam. Unbelievable. That was a 10!

Not only a leaper, Jordan was a truly great scorer. He led the NBA in scoring 10 times and is the all-time leading scorer in the playoffs. Also superb on defense, Jordan is revered as the game's ultimate competitor. He would sacrifice anything required to win and expected the same from his teammates.

BULLS

MICHAEL JORDAN
▶ Shooting Guard

HEIGHT: 6-6   **WEIGHT:** 215 lbs.
BORN: 2/17/1963 in Brooklyn, N.Y.
SCOUTING REPORT: Considered by many the G.O.A.T. of the NBA. Greatest Of All Time! High flyer. Cunning. Steely competitor and winner. A legend.

The only player other than Jordan to lead the NBA in scoring at least seven years in a row was a muscular 7-foot-1 center named ▶ **Wilt Chamberlain**. The Big Dipper's pro career ran from 1959 to 1973, and he set many of the scoring records that Jordan challenged.

Some of Chamberlain's records can't be touched. In 1961–62 Chamberlain averaged more than 50 points per game, which no other player has come close to. He averaged more than 25 rebounds per game in a season three times, which no one else has done even once. Most famously, Chamberlain is the only player in NBA history to score 100 points in a single game. After his career Chamberlain became one of the first NBA stars to appear in Hollywood films.

Even magnificent scorers like Jordan and Chamberlain need help fine-tuning their games. This is where coaches come in. The bedrock of teams that play winning basketball is a strong coach-player connection.

▶ **Forrest "Phog" Allen** was the coach at Kansas University when Wilt Chamberlain came to school in 1956. Nicknamed Phog for his deep, foghorn-like voice, Allen was a master strategist and found creative ways to win. He took Chamberlain, a gifted player, and stretched the role a center might play.

For 50 years Phog Allen coached basketball, and certainly he had

WARRIORS
WILT CHAMBERLAIN
▶ Center

HEIGHT: 7-1   **WEIGHT:** 275 lbs.
BORN: 8/21/1936 in Philadelphia, Pa.
SCOUTING REPORT: One of the most dominant and spectacular big men of all time. The first black basketball superstar. Impossible to stop. Takes over game both offensively and on D.

PHOG ALLEN
▶ Coach and Innovator

10

BORN: 11/18/1885 in Jamesport, Mo.
TEAMS: Kansas University, 1907–09 and 1919–56
SCOUTING REPORT: Innovative coach who shows ability to use players in different capacity and change with the times. Loyal and brilliant. Shows long-term grit.

to be adaptable to prosper for that long. Allen specialized in building relationships with players, administrators, and the public. He even influenced the scheduling of the games to create matchups the public might love. When Allen retired in 1956, he had won more basketball games than any coach in history. People trusted Allen, and that made him great.

Allen himself had played basketball at Kansas under none other than ▶ **Dr. James Naismith**. Born in Canada, Naismith immigrated to the United States and invented the game of basketball in 1891 in Springfield, Massachusetts. His original goal was to create a fun indoor game for his physical education students that could be played during the cold Massachusetts winters. Naismith's game would also promote teamwork, burn off excess energy, and help avoid injurious contact.

The first games played in 1891 had a peach basket hung so high on the wall that no one could think of defending the rim or doing a modern-day slam dunk. Just seven years after hanging the first peach baskets, Naismith began coaching the first basketball program in American history at Kansas University.

Naismith did not gain material riches from his invention but was happy to give this gift to the world. Naismith once said, "I am sure that no man can derive more pleasure from money or power than I do from seeing a pair of basketball goals in some out-of-the-way place." To be truly great, you have to be original and have unique ideas. Basketball was the unique idea of the very original Dr. James Naismith.

JAMES NAISMITH
▶ Inventor and Coach

BORN: 11/6/1861 in Almonte, Canada
TEAM: Kansas University, 1898–1907
SCOUTING REPORT: Creative genius who experiments widely to find the greatest game on Earth. Caring, thoughtful, and responsible citizen.

CHAPTER TWO

PETE MARAVICH
Flashy point guard who once wore Celtic green and white, like Cousy.

BOB COUSY
A Boston Celtic point guard, like Rondo.

RICKY RUBIO
Spanish point guard nicknamed "La Pistola" after "Pistol" Pete Maravich.

SIX DEGREES
OF RAJON RONDO

EARVIN "MAGIC" JOHNSON
Magical point guard was the childhood idol of Rubio.

JASON KIDD
Grew up in California, where Magic spent his entire pro career with the Lakers.

PLEASING PASSERS

A fantastic pass that leads to a score brings a crowd to its feet. Thus a flashy passer who has the vision required to find and hit the open teammate is totally valuable. These creative players see and do things on the court that regular players can't imagine. They make the crowd go, *Ahhh!*

▶ **Rajon Rondo** is an All-Star guard who led the NBA in assists per game in 2011–12 and 2012–13. He is wiry of body and super quick. What is amazing about Rondo's passing game is his ability to stay under control at ultra-high speeds, especially in fast-break situations.

At a lean 6-foot-1, Rondo often has to drive the lane and enter the land of the giants. With long arms and sure hands, Rondo is fearless as he finds a way to distribute the ball in tight spaces.

"When one guy has it going as far as passing the ball, it's contagious," Rondo once said after passing out 18 assists in a game during which his team had 38 assists. This shows how good, creative passing leads to unselfish play—and to winning basketball.

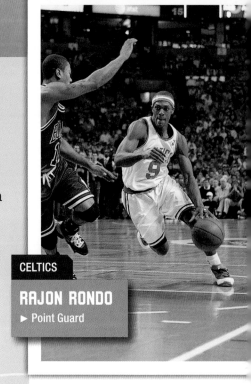

CELTICS

RAJON RONDO
▶ Point Guard

HEIGHT: 6-1   WEIGHT: 186 lbs.
BORN: 2/22/1986 in Louisville, Ken.
SCOUTING REPORT: Speedy and tough ballhandler. Can get his own points or beat you with the pass. Solid shooter and excellent playmaker

The first man to become a star in the NBA mostly because of his passing skills was another Boston Celtic guard named ▶ **Bob Cousy**. He entered the NBA in 1950 and brought an excitement to the court that the game badly needed.

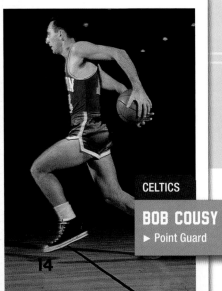

CELTICS

BOB COUSY
▶ Point Guard

HEIGHT: 6-1   WEIGHT: 175 lbs.
BORN: 8/9/1928 in Manhattan, N.Y.
SCOUTING REPORT: Can amaze with ballhandling ability and literally dribble circles around opponents. Gets the ball to the right people almost every time. Fearless shooter.

Because Cousy had broken his dominant arm as a boy, he learned to use his other arm just as well. In this way, he became proficient at using both hands for dribbling and passing. He could dribble his way in and out of any sort of trouble the defense threw at him in order to create the passing angles he needed.

Children all over the country started trying to pass the ball like Cousy, who often gave fakes with his hands, eyes, or the ball. Coaches at that time even complained that young people were trying to be too showy by throwing passes behind the back or neck like Cousy.

One more Celtic that must be mentioned in any discussion of flashy passers is the legendary ▸ **"Pistol" Pete Maravich**. First drafted into the NBA by the Atlanta Hawks in 1970, Maravich also played for the New Orleans Jazz. He grew up as a coach's son, and his drilling and practice techniques have been emulated for years. Maravich's specialty was to get players to believe the ball was going one place and then surprise them with misdirection. We now commonly call this "no-look" passing.

One such move that Maravich became known for was called the slap pass. While running full speed, Maravich would hesitate and let the ball bounce high. At the last second, Maravich used one of his hands to quickly slap the pass left or right to a waiting teammate. Bingo!

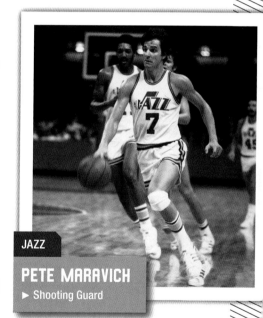

JAZZ

PETE MARAVICH
▸ Shooting Guard

HEIGHT: 6-5   WEIGHT: 197 lbs.
BORN: 6/22/1947 in Aliquippa, Pa.
SCOUTING REPORT: Has the ball on a string. Astonishing dribbler and assist king. Super shooter and scorer, but can totally break your nose if you are not ready for the pass!

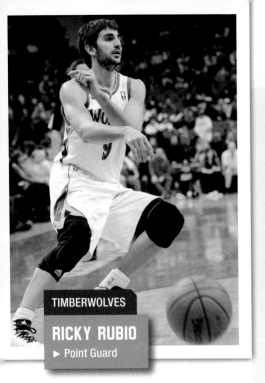

TIMBERWOLVES

RICKY RUBIO

▶ Point Guard

HEIGHT: 6-4   WEIGHT: 185 lbs.
BORN: 10/21/1990 in Barcelona, Spain
SCOUTING REPORT: Gambles on offense and defense, but gambles often pay off. Super creative passer will throw it on a bounce, one-handed, or on the dead run for alley-oops.

▶ **Ricky Rubio**, nicknamed "La Pistola" after Pete Maravich, hails from Spain. He first came to play for the Minnesota Timberwolves in 2011 after playing professional ball for Spanish teams starting at age 14. Like many modern teenagers, Rubio studied the game on YouTube, watching game clips and instructional videos.

Rubio has a knack for seeing openings before they develop. Already he's become well known for embarrassing the defense with a swift, one-handed bounce pass fired between his defender's legs. On defense Rubio uses this anticipation to take plenty of charges, and in 2013–14 he led the league in overall steals. But his passing skills are a gift everyone has recognized as special since his youth.

The 6-foot-4 Rubio is a tall guard, but the player he idolized growing up was even taller. **Earvin** ▶ **"Magic" Johnson** was easily the tallest point guard many people had ever seen. At 6-foot-9 Magic could score inside with post moves just as easily as he could sprint the floor and dish or dunk. A flashy passer, Johnson used his height well. From the top of the key and wings, he could spot players rolling open and fire the ball into the post.

Magic lived for the open court. His size and speed turned ankles on defenders all up and down the hardwood as he led the Los Angeles

HEIGHT: 6-9   WEIGHT: 220 lbs.
BORN: 8/14/1959 in Lansing, Mich.
SCOUTING REPORT: With a forward's size at the point, can play all positions on the court, even center. Uncanny passer shows true genius in the open floor by dishing magical assists to lucky teammates.

Lakers' famous "Showtime" fast break. His unselfish play truly seemed like magic and helped his Lakers to five championships in the 1980s.

So many young players learned to love and play the game from Magic Johnson. A young ▶ **Jason Kidd** did the same, and what he saw was a player capable of putting up a triple-double each time he played. Over 19 years in the NBA, Kidd racked up 107 triple-doubles. In league history, only Magic Johnson (138 triple-doubles) and Oscar Robertson (181 triple-doubles) had more.

Kidd was a deceptive and an effective passer in all phases of the game. On fast breaks he used his strong body to suck defenders to him on drives to the basket before delivering the ball to a trailing teammate. Because point guards are often taught not to drive too deeply in the lane, this was a unique feature of Kidd's game. It often resulted in thundering dunks for Kidd's teammates.

HEIGHT: 6-4   WEIGHT: 210 lbs.
BORN: 3/23/1973 in San Francisco, Calif.
SCOUTING REPORT: Constantly learns and evolves. Serviceable outside shooter. Plays and passes at breakneck speed. Excellent team player and leader.

CHAPTER THREE

ALONZO MOURNING
Played four years at
Georgetown University,
as did Hibbert.

ROY HIBBERT
Squared off against Davis in
2014 All-Star Game.

DIKEMBE MUTUMBO
Patrolled paint alongside
teammate Mourning at
Georgetown University.

SIX DEGREES
OF ANTHONY DAVIS

PATRICK EWING
One of the first remarkable
Georgetown big men, succeeded
by Mutombo and Mourning.

BILL RUSSELL
Wore number six jersey, which Ewing
(normally number 33) wore in final
NBA season to honor Russell.

BIG TIME BLOCKERS

Every player knows that as long as he can squeeze off a shot, he'll have a chance to score. Therefore, the only sure way to totally deny a scoring chance is to block that shot before it ever gets a chance to swish through the net or roll around the rim. That's what this chapter is about: big-time blockers!

A timely blocked shot can change the whole momentum of a close contest. After leaving the University of Kentucky as an NCAA champion, ▸ **Anthony Davis** was named 2012–13 NBA Rookie of the Year for his combination of scoring and spectacular defensive skills.

Davis is a rare athlete. He has a wingspan of 7-foot-8, longer than most centers, but he plays the forward position and gets his blocks all over the floor. Davis is quick enough to switch onto smaller players and is known for extending his improbably long arms to block even three-point jumpers. Indeed, he led the NBA with 2.8 blocks per game in 2013–14.

PELICANS

ANTHONY DAVIS
▸ Center

HEIGHT: 6-10   WEIGHT: 237 lbs.
BORN: 3/11/1993 in Chicago, Ill.
SCOUTING REPORT: Rising young star is long and super athletic. Hands like wild birds. Great hops and timing. Building a solid offensive game as well.

The same year that Davis joined the NBA as a New Orleans Pelican, ▸ **Roy Hibbert** of the Indiana Pacers anchored a defense that helped his team nearly topple eventual NBA-champ Miami in the playoffs. Showing early talent as an offensive rebounder, Hibbert refined his shot-blocking skills and is now annually among the NBA leaders in blocks.

Hibbert is 7-foot-2 and nearly 300 pounds. Ox-strong, he specializes in jumping straight up to meet driving opponents. These types of clean blocks right at the basket are special, and Hibbert is strong enough to stop slam-dunks cold.

PACERS

ROY HIBBERT
▶ Center

HEIGHT: 7-2   WEIGHT: 290 lbs.
BORN: 12/11/1986 in Queens, N.Y.
SCOUTING REPORT: Protects the rim like it's his home. Very tough defender loves to mix it up inside and fight for blocks and rebounds.

Hibbert entered the NBA in 2008 after four years of college at Georgetown University.

Another Georgetown alumnus is ▶ **Alonzo Mourning**. "Zo," as Mourning was affectionately called, was a defensive stalwart in the NBA for a long 15-year career with the Charlotte Hornets, New Jersey Nets, and Miami Heat. In 2014 he was honored with an induction into the Basketball Hall of Fame.

Zo presented an intimidating wall in the lane, but his outstanding quality as a blocker was his consistency and perseverance. Mourning tried never to be out of position and was extra patient in waiting for the moment when he could turn the emotion of a game with a crucial block. Some defenders are constantly leaving their feet, leaping too early for the block and getting caught in the air. Not Zo. He was all about timing.

HEAT

ALONZO MOURNING
▶ Center

HEIGHT: 6-10   WEIGHT: 240 lbs.
BORN: 2/8/1970 in Chesapeake, Va.
SCOUTING REPORT: Waits with patience and then explodes on defense. Great personality and plays with passion. Leader. Tough as nails.

21

DIKEMBE MUTUMBO
▶ Center

HEIGHT: 7-2   WEIGHT: 260 lbs.
BORN: 6/25/1966 in Kinshasa, The
Republic of Congo
SCOUTING REPORT: Charismatic, lean, and
determined player can change the whole
game with one block. And one wag!

▶ **Dikembe Mutombo** was another player to come to NBA from the long line of defensive stoppers trained by Coach John Thompson at Georgetown. The Hoyas took great pride in low-scoring contests and in being tougher defensively than almost any other college team in the land.

Mutumbo came to Georgetown from The Republic of Congo in Africa and evolved into more of a showman in the NBA than anyone expected. For a player who spoke little English early on, Mutumbo said plenty with his actions. He swatted leather from the get-go and was named NBA Defensive Player of the Year four times in his career.

The finger wag was Mutumbo's signature gesture. It let the other team and the crowd know that if you are going to mess with Mutumbo, you might have the ball batted up into the stands for your trouble. Wag!

Before Mutumbo and Mourning, who were college teammates at Georgetown, came the great ▶ **Patrick Ewing**. Not only a cunning shot blocker, Ewing was an enforcer for four years at Georgetown, and then for 15 seasons with the New York Knicks. To stir some fear, he would goaltend on a shot or swat a layup attempt far into the seats.

KNICKS

PATRICK EWING
▶ Center

HEIGHT: 7-0   **WEIGHT:** 240 lbs.
BORN: 8/5/1962 in Kingston, Jamaica
SCOUTING REPORT: Can get blocks even after shooter passes him by. Solid scorer and rebounder who always shows up ready to play. Uses his intelligence as much as his body to win battles.

Ewing, who was born in Jamaica and lived there until age 12, grew to a stout seven feet tall and had a scowl that seemed set in granite. This scowl mentally "blocked" many an opposing shooter. It planted the seed that maybe he was better off not shooting than to shoot and be humiliated.

Another intimidating pro was ▶ **Bill Russell**, a Boston Celtic from 1956 to 1969. The first African-American superstar in the NBA, Russell displayed deft instincts and intelligence on the court. Russell knew that to defend well, one must deny a scorer his favorite spots.

Russell knew that winning the mental game was also key to success. "The idea is not to block every shot," he once famously said. "The idea is to make your opponent believe you might block every shot."

Eloquent off the court, Russell was a terror on it. Russell had the height of a center but the footspeed of a guard. Running the court at breakneck speed, he perfectly complemented Bob Cousy and his Celtic teammates. They won an astonishing 11 NBA Championships.

CELTICS

BILL RUSSELL
▶ Center

HEIGHT: 6-10   **WEIGHT:** 215 lbs.
BORN: 2/12/1934 in West Monroe, La.
SCOUTING REPORT: Slender, but good luck trying to move him around. Super smart with an unmatched work ethic on the court. Burns with talent and fire for the game.

CHAPTER FOUR

RAY ALLEN
All-time three-pointers leader born in California, like Lillard.

DAMIAN LILLARD
Made first All-Star Game apprearance in 2014, as did Curry.

REGGIE MILLER
Held 3-point scoring record before Allen broke it.

SIX DEGREES
OF STEPHEN CURRY

LARRY BIRD
Many battles with Miller in playoffs and All-Star Game three-point shootouts.

FRED BROWN
Received many a SuperSonic pass from point guard Dennis Johnson, who later passed to Bird in Beantown.

MAGNIFICENT MARKSMEN

The lane can be a rugged place in pro basketball. Thus, many of the best shooters have claimed a domain of their own, and that place is beyond the three-point line. These marksmen leap high up—where the air is thin and the lights are bright—to launch their missiles from afar. Now, listen closely. Swish!

WARRIORS

STEPHEN CURRY
▶ Point Guard

HEIGHT: 6-3   WEIGHT: 185 lbs.
BORN: 3/14/1988 in Akron, Ohio
SCOUTING REPORT: One of the most feared shooters
in the NBA. Seemingly limitless range. Can shoot off
the bounce and has an incredible step-back jumper.

▶ **Stephen Curry** of the Golden State Warriors set an NBA record by making 272 triples during the 2012–13 season. Curry is unquestionably the best outside bomber in the league, and every opponent knows this. If he's left open, opponents might as well be giving him a layup. So Curry is not often left alone.

What makes Curry so effective is his handle and ability to create space to shoot. Unlike many shooters, Curry is deadly both in a catch-and-shoot situation, when he is standing still, and when he comes off a dribble move. His release is lightning quick. Three!

Another young player who joined Curry as a first-time All-Star in 2014 is ▶ **Damian Lillard** of the Portland Trail Blazers. One of the debates over these two amazing shooters is about which one has the best step-back jumper. Curry is so famous for his that some people call it a Steph-back jumper.

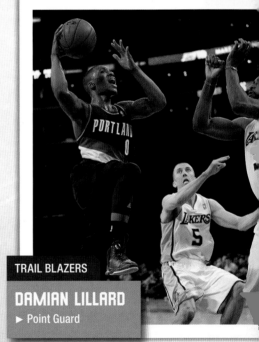

TRAIL BLAZERS

DAMIAN LILLARD
▶ Point Guard

HEIGHT: 6-3   WEIGHT: 195 lbs.
BORN: 7/15/1990 in Oakland, Calif.
SCOUTING REPORT: Coming from a lesser collegiate power, has shown leaps and bounds of growth. Efficient scorer who takes care of the ball. Fearless shooter who wants to win.

Yet Lillard is worthy competition, as his footspeed is rarely matched among NBA shooting guards. Although he and Curry are both 6-foot-3, Lillard packs about 15 pounds more. Lillard is a point guard who moves like a lightning-charged pinball. He rolls past defenders with his fearless drives and lights the scoreboard with clutch shooting. Lillard makes a way where there seems no way.

While Lillard and Curry are both fairly new to the NBA, the all-time three-point leader is the impeccable sharpshooter ▶ **Ray Allen**. Allen is 6-foot-5 and has a silky smooth jump shot that is the envy of many other guards. From his perfectly shaved head to the laces of his shoes, Allen is a smooth shooter.

Known for his preparation, Allen is compulsive in the routines he follows. He follows a strict pattern in warm-ups and works hard to make his incredible range expand. Basically once Allen passes half-court, he's a threat. Allen has canned nearly 3,000 threeballs since entering the league in 1996. That's 9,000 points just on threes! Incredible.

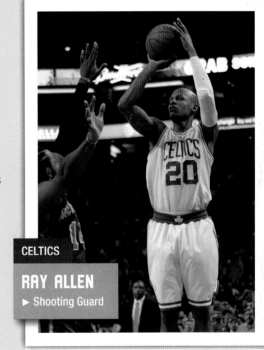

CELTICS

RAY ALLEN
▶ Shooting Guard

HEIGHT: 6-5   WEIGHT: 205 lbs.
BORN: 7/20/1975 in Merced, Calif.
SCOUTING REPORT: Cannot leave this man open. Lives to take last shots and especially thrives in pressure situations and postseason. A winner!

PACERS

REGGIE MILLER
▶ Shooting Guard

HEIGHT: 6-7   **WEIGHT:** 195 lbs.
BORN: 8/24/1965 in Riverside, Calif.
SCOUTING REPORT: Sharpshooter with a sharp tongue to match. Backs up talk with well-earned endgame reputation. May hit shots seemingly falling into the stands.

The man whose all-time three-point record Allen bested was an Indiana Pacer named ▶ **Reggie Miller**. A slender outside assassin, Miller could lose defenders around a screen, and at 6-foot-7 Miller could shoot over shorter defenders.

What he was best known for was his ability in the clutch. In his playoff career alone, Miller sank 320 triples, and once again, only Ray Allen has made more. Most famously, Miller torched the Knicks for an amazing eight points—including two three-pointers—in just nine seconds to cap off a comeback win at the end of Game 1 of the 1995 Eastern Conference Semifinals. Eighteen sweet-shooting NBA seasons, all spent with Indiana, made Miller a true Pacer legend.

Yet as legends go, few are more heralded than forward ▶ **Larry Bird** of the Boston Celtics. Like Miller, Bird played his entire career, 13 seasons, with one team, leading Boston to three NBA titles.

Bird, at 6-foot-10, shocked the league with his ability to score inside and outside. No player of his height before him showed such an uncanny ability to anticipate. Bird made many plays before anyone saw they were possible. Vision!

An Indiana native, Bird became an NBA legend despite having little speed or jumping ability. His instincts for the game were

CELTICS

LARRY BIRD
▶ Forward

unmatched. Bird knew just when he could get his shot off and how to square his body to shoot. He knew that the key to being a good shooter is having the proper balance.

Bird played for years with backcourt mate Dennis Johnson, who also once fed passes to another famous long-range gunner named ▶ **"Downtown" Freddy Brown**. With a name like that, who could forget the man who led the NBA in three-point shooting percentage in 1979–80, the first year the NBA added the three-point stripe?

Freddy Brown, like Bird, played all 13 of his seasons with one team: the Seattle SuperSonics. Brown lived up to his name in Seattle, launching shots from beyond the business district. Number 32 for the green and gold could ring up the points en masse, and the fans loved to ring up his great rhyming name. *It's another three for Downtown Freddy Brown!*

SUPERSONICS

FRED BROWN
▶ Shooting Guard

CHAPTER FIVE

KEVIN LOVE
Gold medal-winning U.S. Olympic teammate of Anthony in 2012.

CARMELO ANTHONY
Won 2012–13 NBA scoring title to break up three-year run of Durant's.

KOBE BRYANT
Fellow Californian with Love and also U.S. Olympic teammates.

SIX DEGREES
OF KEVIN DURANT

KARL MALONE
Jazz legend played final season of long career as a Laker alongside Bryant.

KAREEM ABDUL-JABBAR
The only man above Malone on the all-time NBA scorers list.

SPLENDID SCORERS

To become a top scorer, even a very gifted player must find a way to make points in games when the defense is doubling him or the rim feels miles away. How? By being creative. This chapter showcases some of the most inventive and determined scorers in NBA history.

HEIGHT: 6-9   WEIGHT: 240 lbs.
BORN: 9/29/1988 in Washington, D.C.
SCOUTING REPORT: Built to score and impossible to stop. Will get his points but is also a great team player. Admired and respected league-wide, Durant can tear up any defense.

A lean and tough 6-foot-9 forward named ▶ **Kevin Durant** of the Oklahoma City Thunder is the top scorer in the NBA today. The 2013-14 season marked the fifth straight season that Durant led the NBA in total points scored. He also captured the 2013–14 MVP award, his first such honor.

Durant is an absolute dead-eye shooter, but he combines that touch with a fearless slash-to-the-basket mentality. Often, all defenders can do to slow him down is foul him, but—like many great scorers—Durant rarely misses free throws. Game in and game out, opponents must pick their poison in defending him. If the defense concentrates too much on Durant's outside game, he'll go by them, and they'll be watching him soar for a dunk with half his arm above the rim.

Durant teamed with another high-scoring forward named ▶ **Carmelo Anthony** to lead the U.S. Olympic men's basketball team to a gold medal in 2008. Both Anthony and Durant were drafted after only one year of

HEIGHT: 6-8   WEIGHT: 235
BORN: 5/29/1984 in Brooklyn, N.Y.
SCOUTING REPORT: Long limbs make for high shot release that's hard to block. Can play with back to basket or face up with great range. Very difficult to stop one-on-one.

college ball. They represent the only two teenagers to average better than 20 points per game as rookies in the history of the NBA.

Anthony is a good enough shooter to make defenders cover the three, but he is especially dangerous backing into the post or attacking the rim. Anthony stands 6-foot-8 but has the wingspan of a 7-footer. He loves to use his length and pump fakes to get defenders to leave their feet so he can spring skyward to unleash his silky jumper.

▶ **Kevin Love** teamed with Anthony on the 2008 Olympic team and made life very tough for defenses. A bit heavy in college, Love transformed his 6-foot-10 frame into a leaner package that has made him into a terror on the boards. Love went to Cleveland in 2014 after spending his first six years with the Timberwolves in Minnesota where he gained a reputation as a relentless rebounder.

K-Love gets many of his points on dogged offensive putbacks, timing nearly every leap perfectly. He is also a master of positioning and great footwork. Love's charm doesn't stop under the boards as his outside shot is also potent. In 2013–14 he set the Timberwolves franchise record for most threeballs in a season with 190.

CAVALIERS

KEVIN LOVE
▶ Power Forward

HEIGHT: 6-10   WEIGHT: 243 lbs.
BORN: 9/7/1988 in Santa Monica, Calif.
SCOUTING REPORT: Rare blend of top-flight rebounding and scoring. Has developed a deep shot that must be respected. Good passer who excels at the full-court outlet pass.

Also teaming with Love on the 2012 U.S. Olympic team was long-time NBA star ▸ **Kobe Bryant**. In 1996 Bryant went straight to the NBA from high school. By the age of 23, Bryant had already won a trio of NBA titles with the Lakers alongside star center Shaquille O'Neal.

Bryant is a player who wants to take the shot at the end of the game when all the pressure is on. Amazingly, although the defense prepares to prevent Bryant from scoring, he finds a way to score anyway. He seems to want it more. At 6-foot-6, Bryant has superb physical skills, but his mental toughness and craftiness to create good shots set him apart. He's currently fourth all-time in scoring with a chance to take the top spot if he can stay healthy and keep filling the basket.

Number two on that all-time NBA scoring list is the man who really put the power in power forward: ▸ **Karl Malone**. A Utah Jazz fan favorite, Malone delivered points so regularly he was called "The Mailman."

A rugged 6-foot-9 and 260 pounds, Malone scored most of his points down low in the paint.

LAKERS
KOBE BRYANT
▸ Shooting Guard

HEIGHT: 6-6   WEIGHT: 205 lbs.
BORN: 8/26/1978 in Philadelphia, Pa.
SCOUTING REPORT: Tireless worker sets high standard for teammates. Scores from anywhere on floor. Great athlete, but mental edge sets him apart.

JAZZ
KARL MALONE
▸ Power Forward

HEIGHT: 6-9   WEIGHT: 255 lbs.
BORN: 07/24/1963 in Summerfield, La.
SCOUTING REPORT: The Mailman delivers. Reliable as sun and wind. Brutally efficient scorer who has mid-range accuracy but can bang inside with the best. Strong!

He could also stick his patented mid-range jump shot or score off the pick and roll with point guard John Stockton, Malone's teammate in Utah for 18 season who loved passing the rock to his big man. Oft-fouled, Malone both attempted (13,188) and made (9,787) more free throws than anyone in NBA history and finished second in career points.

Topping Malone as the NBA's all-time leading scorer is center ▶ **Kareem Abdul-Jabbar**. The towering center scored 38,387 points and won six championships while playing for the Milwaukee Bucks (6 seasons) and Lakers (14 seasons) from 1969 to 1989. Always lean and in-shape, Kareem was so cool and unflappable that he was as dependable as sunshine in California.

Kareem Abdul-Jabbar's name is almost synonymous with an unblockable shot called the Sky Hook. Yet to think of him as only a scorer is dead wrong. Abdul-Jabbar finished his career in the top three all-time in rebounds and blocks and was an uncanny passer, dealing assists all over the court with his keen vision. Many consider Abdul-Jabbar the greatest player of all-time. Without a doubt, he was the ultimate scorer.

LAKERS

KAREEM ABDUL-JABBAR
▶ Center

HEIGHT: 7-2   WEIGHT: 225 lbs.
BORN: 4/16/1947 in New York, N.Y.
SCOUTING REPORT: One of the greatest to ever play possesses indefensible Sky Hook, launched with either hand. If he gets the ball on the block, he's very likely to convert. Great passer and intelligent teammate plays D and knows how to win.

CHAPTER SIX

TONY PARKER
Western Conference point guard
rival of Nash's for 13 years.

STEVE NASH
Teammate of Nowitzki in Dallas
from 1998–2004, and also only
other foreign-born MVP.

YAO MING
Father played professional
basketball, as did Parker's.

SIX DEGREES
OF DIRK NOWITZKI

MANU GINOBILI
On way to gold at 2004
Olympic Games, helped
Argentina to 82-57 win
over China, led by Yao.

VLADE DIVAC
Helped Yugoslavia to OT victory over
Ginobili's Argentina in the 2002 FIBA
World Championship title game.

GLOBAL GAMERS

We have learned about basketball's roots and Dr. James Naismith. An immigrant from Canada, Naismith came to the United States and invented the game to try to promote teamwork, exercise, civility, and creativity. Now, more than 100 years later, we see basketball, with its wonderful qualities, being played all over the world. We now also enjoy many exciting foreign-born stars in the NBA. Welcome, friends.

HEIGHT: 7-0   WEIGHT: 245 lbs.
BORN: 6/19/1978 in Wurzburg, West Germany
SCOUTING REPORT: Length and high release-point makes shot unblockable, and arsenal of shots extends from the lane to far beyond the three. A complete scorer.

Longtime Dallas Maverick ► **Dirk Nowitzki** was born and raised in Germany. Blond-haired and rangy, Nowitzki possesses perhaps the best outside shooting touch ever for a player of seven feet. After being drafted to the NBA in 1998, he became a perennial All-Star, won the NBA Most Valuable Player in 2007, and led the Mavericks to the NBA title in 2011.

MAVERICKS

DIRK NOWITZKI
► Power Forward

Inside or at mid-range, Dirk is famous for shooting unorthodox shots that might be taken off balance, fading away, or even off one leg! Nowitzki exemplifies the rising popularity of basketball in Western Europe in the decades after World War II. Concrete outdoor courts and indoor gyms became more commonplace as the sport grew in countries such as Germany, France, Spain, and Italy.

Nowitzki and the Mavs even played a game in Berlin in 2012, dedicating an outdoor court to encourage German youth to play the game.

Nowitzki's earned tremendous respect over his long career. He's more than just the best German player to ever lace up high-tops. No less than Kobe Bryant said, "Dirk Nowitzki is the best foreign player of all time, period."

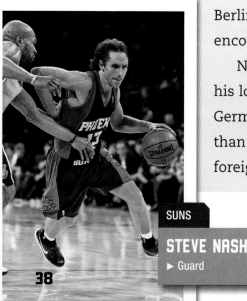

SUNS

STEVE NASH
► Guard

HEIGHT: 6-3   WEIGHT: 178 lbs.
BORN: 2/7/1984 in Johannesburg, South Africa
SCOUTING REPORT: Ball-handling skills are dizzying and impossible. Creates unbelievable passing angles. Tough and supersmart with deadly accurate shot.

Nowitzki's point guard and running mate for many years at Dallas was ▸ **Steve Nash**. Nash was born in South Africa and raised in Canada. Slender and 6-foot-3, Nash has deft instincts as a passer and shooter and seems to see possibilities many others do not. He specializes in long-range bombs, floaters lofted in the lane, and nifty, precise bounce passes. His ball-handling is so good that it seems at times as if Nash has the ball on a string like a yo-yo.

As a Phoenix Sun, Nash won back-to-back MVPs in 2006 and 2007, and he and Nowitzki are the only two foreign-born players to win this prestigious recognition.

In the NBA Western Conference, Nash and San Antonio Spur ▸ **Tony Parker** have fought many battles. As famous as Nash is in Canada, Parker is in France, where he started playing professionally at age 15. Parker is cat-quick and is absolutely fearless in driving the lane. On the dead run he can accomplish a spin move or pull up for his famous teardrop jumper, arcing the ball softly above defenders and letting it float down for a key bucket.

SPURS

TONY PARKER
▸ Point Guard

HEIGHT: 6-2 WEIGHT: 185 lbs.
BORN: 5/17/1982 in Bruges, Belgium
SCOUTING REPORT: Fluid and lightning fast but has the balance of a steeplejack racer. A champion whose team comes first. Teardrop shot on the run is a thing of beauty.

Entering the league in 2001, Parker has since led the Spurs to four NBA titles. Despite playing with an injury, Parker helped the Spurs play a share-the-ball brand of team basketball that steamrolled all playoff opponents in 2014.

YAO MING
▶ Center

HEIGHT: 7-6   WEIGHT: 310 lbs.
BORN: 9/12/1980 in Shanghai, China
SCOUTING REPORT: Fan favorite. Superior coordination and timing for someone so tall. Dominant on both offense and defense. When not injured, a true force.

When basketball is played with such grace and flair, the game is addictive to play and watch. Parker has fought many battles with in-state rival Houston in his career. The Rockets boasted arguably the most influential foreign star of all-time in their giant center from China, ▶ **Yao Ming**.

Yao entered the NBA as the first pick in 2002, and the booming popularity of the game in China today is directly connected. Suddenly, the home of 1.3 billion of the Earth's people began paying more attention to basketball.

Yao Ming was huge but agile at 7-foot-6. Yet at first Yao had to be encouraged to dunk, as he didn't want to show up his opponents. His open, engaging personality and great sense of humor helped him gain American fans very quickly, though his NBA career lasted only eight seasons due to foot injuries. David Stern, former NBA commissioner, said of Yao, "He became a bridge builder between our two countries and inspired millions of potential basketball players around the world."

▶ **Manu Ginobili** played in the same NBA division and in the same Olympic Games as Yao Ming when Argentina

SPURS

MANU GINOBILI
▶ Guard-Forward

HEIGHT: 6-6   WEIGHT: 205 lbs.
BORN: 07/28/1977 in Buenos Aires, Argentina
SCOUTING REPORT: Difficult to stop with driving "Euro-Step" move. Wiry with man-strength to battle inside. Competitive and burns to win. Great team player.

won gold in 2004. Ginobili personified the versatile and cooperative nature of his Argentinian team that led to this landmark win.

Ginobili is one of the greatest steals in the history of the NBA Draft, as the 6-foot-6 shooting guard was picked 57th overall in 1999. He would later win four titles with Tony Parker and Tim Duncan on the Spurs, and he is one of only two players ever to have won NBA, Euroleague, and Olympic titles. A crafty and daring shooter and passer, Ginobili's a winner.

▶ **Vlade Divac** played center in the tough Western Conference for both the Lakers and the Kings in his career, facing Ginobili's Spurs many times. He is one of those rare players who we know by just his first name—Vlade!—and this shows his extreme popularity.

Vlade was one of the first foreign stars to have a huge influence in the NBA. He was drafted out of the former Yugoslavia in 1989 by the Lakers. The NBA had previously viewed European players as too soft or not skilled enough to compete, but Vlade helped change that perception.

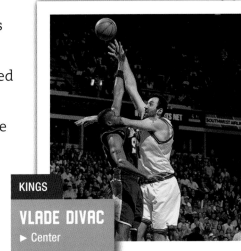

KINGS

VLADE DIVAC
▶ Center

His totals for points, rebounds, blocks, and assists rank highly among the top NBA centers of all time. But Vlade was best known for his engaging and emotional personality, and for being a great teammate. He loved to make his teammates better with his deft passing skills. Because he left home at 14 to pursue his career, basketball became like another family to Vlade. The players and fans he met doing what he loved were his connection to the world.

HEIGHT: 7-1   WEIGHT: 243 lbs.
BORN: 02/03/1968 in Prijepolje, Serbia, SFR Yugoslavia
SCOUTING REPORT: Shows heart, emotion, and fire for teammates. Dives and hustles. Great passing and solid fundamentals make him a true force.

SIX DEGREES TRIVIA ⟩ ⟩ ⟩ ⟩ ⟩

MATCH THE PLAYER WITH HIS NICKNAME:

1.	LeBRON JAMES	LA PISTOLA
2.	MICHAEL JORDAN	THE HICK FROM FRENCH LICK
3.	DWYANE WADE	MOUNT MUTOMBO
4.	WILT CHAMBERLAIN	THE CHOSEN ONE
5.	RICKY RUBIO	ZO
6.	PETE MARAVICH	HIS AIRNESS
7.	BOB COUSY	THE GREAT WALL
8.	KARL MALONE	THE BIG DIPPER
9.	KAREEM ABDUL-JABBAR	THE MAILMAN
10.	LARRY BIRD	PISTOL
11.	FREDDIE BROWN	CAP
12.	DIKEMBE MUTOMBO	HOUDINI OF THE HARDWOOD
13.	PATRICK EWING	FLASH
14.	ALONZO MOURNING	HOYA DESTROYA
15.	YAO MING	DOWNTOWN

Answers:

1. The Chosen One, 2. His Airness, 3. Flash, 4. The Big Dipper, 5. La Pistola, 6. Pistol, 7. Houdini of the Hardwood, 8. The Mailman, 9. Cap, 10. The Hick from French Lick, 11. Downtown, 12. Mount Mutombo, 13. Zo, 14. Hoya Destroya, 15. The Great Wall

42

See if you can guess which NBA team or teams each of the players in our book played for.

New Jersey Nets   Golden State Warriors   Dallas Mavericks
Denver Nuggets   Houston Rockets   New Orleans Hornets/Pelicans
Washington Wizards   Philadelphia/San Francisco Warriors
Atlanta Hawks   New Orleans/Utah Jazz   Milwaukee Bucks
Golden State Warriors   Los Angeles Lakers   Seattle SuperSonics
Cleveland Cavaliers   Oklahoma City Thunder   Philadelphia 76ers
Miami Heat   Orlando Magic   Cincinnati Royals
Indiana Pacers   Phoenix Suns   San Antonio Spurs   Boston Celtics
Minnesota Timberwolves   Charlotte Hornets   New York Knicks
Chicago Bulls   Portland Trail Blazers   Sacramento Kings

LIST OF PLAYERS:

CHAPTER ONE
LeBron James (two teams)
Dwyane Wade (one team)
Michael Jordan (two teams)
Wilt Chamberlain (three teams)
Phog Allen (no NBA affiliation)
James Naismith (no NBA affiliation)

CHAPTER TWO
Rajon Rondo (one team)
Bob Cousy (two teams)
Pete Maravich (three teams)
Ricky Rubio (one team)
Magic Johnson (one team)
Jason Kidd (four teams)

CHAPTER THREE
Roy Hibbert (one team)
Anthony Davis (one team)
Alonzo Mourning (three teams)
Dikembe Mutombo (six teams)
Patrick Ewing (three teams)
Bill Russell (one team)

CHAPTER FOUR
Stephen Curry (one team)
Damian Lillard (one team)
Ray Allen (four teams)
Reggie Miller (one team)
Larry Bird (one team)
Downtown Freddy Brown (one team)

CHAPTER FIVE
Kevin Durant (one team)
Carmelo Anthony (two teams)
Kevin Love (two teams)
Kobe Bryant (one team)
Karl Malone (two teams)
Kareem Abdul-Jabbar (two teams)

CHAPTER SIX
Dirk Nowitzki (one team)
Steve Nash (three teams)
Tony Parker (one team)
Manu Ginobili (one team)
Yao Ming (one team)
Vlade Divac (three teams)

Answers:

Chapter One: James – Cavaliers, Heat; Wade – Heat; Jordan – Bulls, Wizards; Chamberlain – Phil./S.F. Warriors, 76ers, Lakers; Phog Allen – none; Naismith – none **Chapter Two:** Rondo – Celtics; Cousy – Celtics, Royals; Maravich – Hawks, Jazz, Celtics; Rubio – Timberwolves; Johnson – Lakers; Kidd – Mavericks, Suns, Nets, Knicks **Chapter Three:** Hibbert – Pacers; Davis – Hornets/Pelicans; Mourning – Hornets, Heat, Nets; Mutombo – Nuggets, Hawks, 76ers, Nets, Knicks, Rockets, Knicks, SuperSonics; Ewing – Knicks, SuperSonics, Magic; Russell – Celtics **Chapter Four:** Curry – G. S. Warriors; Lillard – Trail Blazers; Ray Allen – Bucks, SuperSonics, Celtics, Heat, Miller – Pacers; Bird – Celtics; Brown – SuperSonics **Chapter Five:** Durant – SuperSonics/Thunder; Anthony – Nuggets, Knicks; Love – Timberwolves, Cavaliers; Bryant – Lakers; Malone – Jazz, Lakers; Abdul-Jabbar – Bucks, Lakers **Chapter Six:** Nowitzki – Mavericks; Nash – Suns – Mavericks, Suns, Mavericks; Parker – Spurs; Ginobili – Spurs; Yao – Rockets; Divac – Lakers, Hornets, Kings

Leading scorers on U.S.
Men's Olympic teams

Players born in
New York state

These players were
all Number 1 picks
in the NBA Draft

Players born
in California

Point guards
with jersey #9

Members of
All-Defensive
1st Team

BILL
RUSSELL

PATRICK
EWING

ROY
HIBBERT

ANTHONY
DAVIS

ALONZO
MOURNING

DIKEMBE
MUTOMBO

JASON
KIDD

ERVIN
"MAGIC"
JOHNSON

BOB
COUSY

RAJON
RONDO

PETE
MARAVICH

RICKY
RUBIO

JAMES
NAISMITH

DWYANE
WADE

LEBRON
JAMES

PHOG
ALLEN

MICHAEL
JORDAN

WILT
CHAMBERLAIN

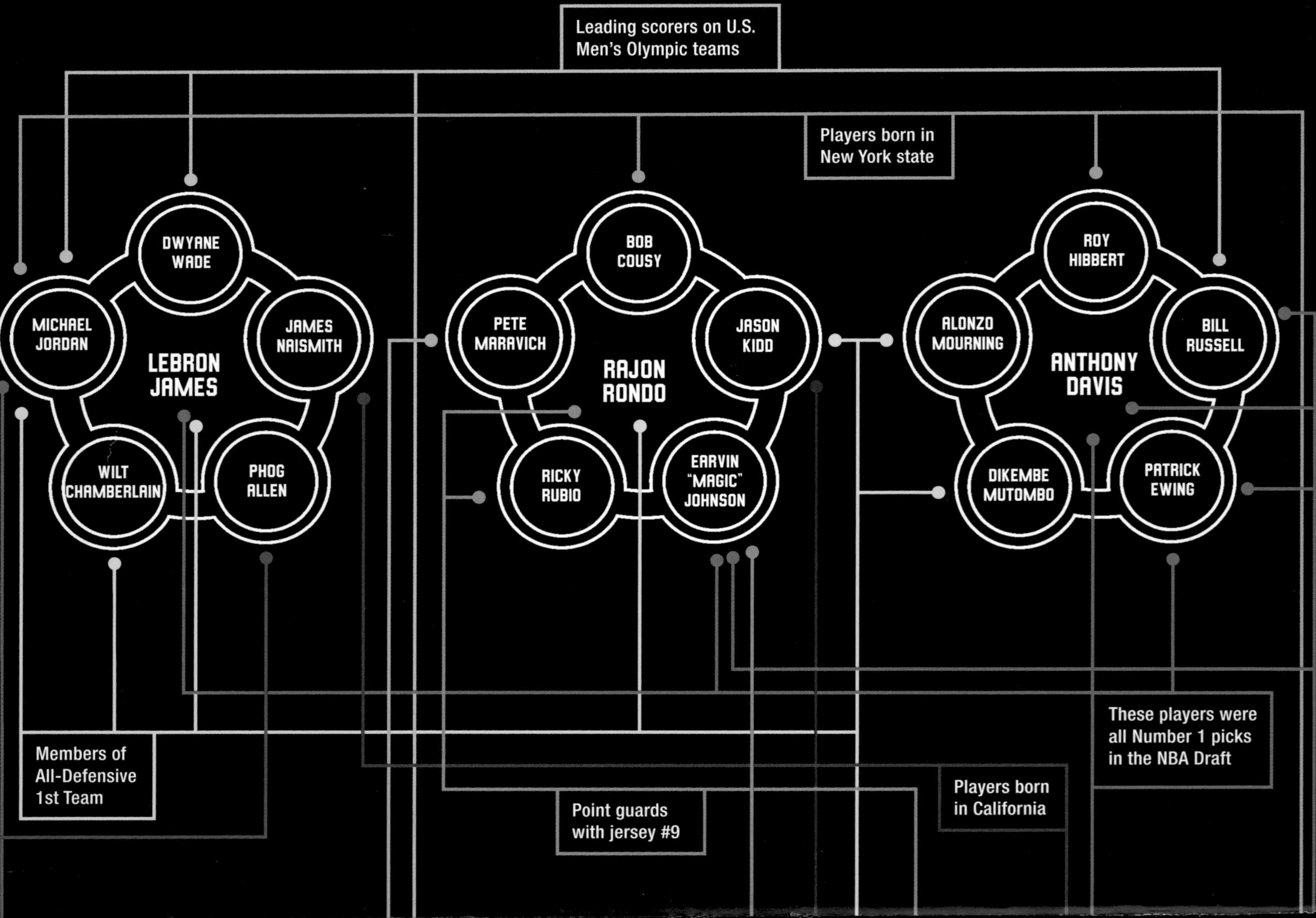

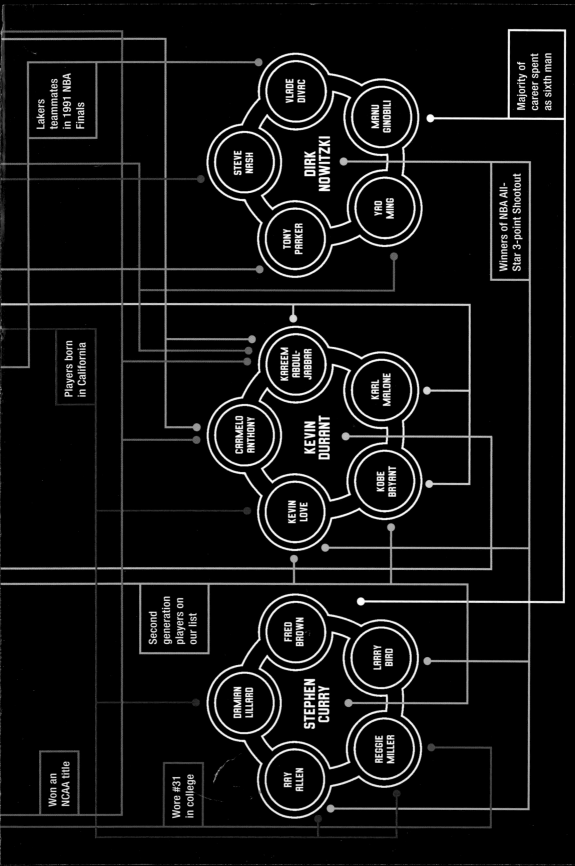

GLOSSARY

arsenal—storehouse of weapons; in basketball, this refers to the variety of skills a player possesses

ball-handling—the skill of dribbling, passing, and protecting the basketball

center—position in basketball involving playing near the basket and usually filled by tallest players; also called post or "five."

consistency—always behaving in the same way

drive—in basketball, an offensive move in which a player dribbles the ball toward the hoop in order to shoot from closer up

fast break—play or method in basketball that involves the offensive team advancing the ball from one end of the court to the other very quickly by way of fast dribbling or passing

forward—position in basketball involving playing both outside and inside; also called wing, "three," "four," or, more specifically, small forward for outside-playing forwards or power forward for inside-playing forwards

immigrant—someone who comes from one country to live in another

influential—to have an effect on someone or something

perseverance—the act of continually committing to a certain action or belief

point guard—position in basketball involving dribbling, passing, shooting, and directing the team and usually filled by smallest, quickest players; also called one-guard, or just "one."

putback—in basketball, the act of getting a rebound and quickly shooting it back into the hoop

range—in basketball, refers to the distance from which a player can comfortably and successfully make shots

relentless—sustained and unyielding; never giving up

shooting guard—position in basketball involving shooting, scoring, and ballhandling on offense; also called off-guard, two-guard, or just "two."

triple-double—feat in basketball where a player achieves double figures in three different areas, such as points, rebounds, and assists

unorthodox—not conforming to rules or modes of normal conduct

vision—the act or power of sensing with the eyes; in basketball, this refers to a player's ability to pass to the open teammate

READ MORE

Kelley, K.C. *2014 Basketball Superstars.* NBA Readers. New York: Scholastic, 2014.

LeBoutillier, Nate. *Play Basketball Like a Pro: Key Skills and Tips.* Play Like the Pros. North Mankato, Minn.: Capstone Press, 2010.

LeBoutillier, Nate. *The Best of Everything Basketball.* All-Time Best of Sports. North Mankato, Minn.: Capstone Press, 2011.

INTERNET SITES

FactHound offers a safe, fun way to find Internet sites related to this book. All of the sites on FactHound have been researched by our staff.

Here's all you do:

Visit *www.facthound.com*

Type in this code: 9781491421444

Check out projects, games and lots more at
www.capstonekids.com

INDEX